MINDFUL
MAGIC

For children Aged 9 to 12 Years Old

MELISSA O'NEILL

Printed in the United States of America
First Printing 2020
First Edition 2020

ISBN: 9798699543670

10 9 8 7 6 5 4 3 2 1

Illustrations by ouahdahoyounes @fiverr.com

This book is dedicated to Brian, who supports me in my journey and passion for spreading mindful ways and love and light to all the children in the world.

TABLE OF CONTENTS

ABOUT THE AUTHOR.. 1

CHAPTER 1 6

MAGICAL GENIE

CHAPTER 2 14

THE MAGIC LAMP

CHAPTER 3 17

CRAZY WAY, CRAZY DAY

CHAPTER 4 23

WHEN THE GOING GETS TOUGH

CHAPTER 5 27

ATTITUDES THAT BRING MAGIC

CHAPTER 6 35

BUILDING THE MAGIC BLOCKS

CHAPTER 7 48

LIGHT BULB MOMENT

CHAPTER 8 55

MINDFUL MAGIC IN PLAY

CHAPTER 9 60

NEW WAYS TO BE

CHAPTER 10 66

A PLEASANT SURPRISE

CHAPTER 11 70

MORE JINGLE JANGLE

CHAPTER 12 77

THE EYE OPENER

ABOUT THE AUTHOR

My name is Melissa O'Neill. I am a meditation and mindfulness teacher and practitioner living in the garden county of Ireland. For many years, I have worked with children and those who have autism and are on the autism spectrum.

Children of all ages can benefit from mindfulness and bringing gentle awareness to the present moment.

I am delighted to introduce this book to children aged 9 to 12 years old. The book is written in an engaging and fun-loving way, and it revolves around a magical genie and a boy called George. George is a headstrong character, and his anger, behaviours, and worries take a toll on him. The genie teaches George how to adapt mindfulness into his day. The nine attitudes of mindfulness, according to Jon Kabat-Zinn, a teacher of mindfulness, is played out in the story. These ways bring George magic that he could not see. The genie and his lamp play a beautiful role in magic, love, and light. George discovers that finding his heart and new ways to cope will help him to become happier and healthier and free.

The theme of mindfulness plays out in the book to bring children knowledge of mindful ways which ultimately can support and help them to show up for themselves in a new light.

The title I chose for the book is *Mindful Magic*.

Mindfulness is magic; just wait and see. Magic happens when you stay with the present and accept life fully.

This book is recommended for 9 to 12-year-olds.

Hi everyone! In this book, you will find mindful magic for all mankind. I have lots of secrets, just wait and see all the magic we can bring to the world, you and me.

This magical journey will bring you to a forever land that never dies—a place of love, freedom, happiness, joy and peace.

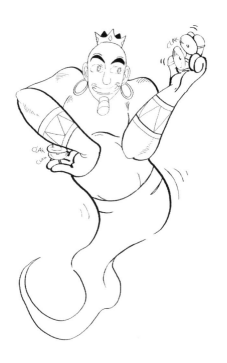

CHAPTER 1

MAGICAL GENIE

The genie holds the lamp in his hands, rubbing its sides as it changes colour.

"Bubble, bubble, fire of light, crimson gold shining bright. Moon and stars, love and light, bring my friend to receive the gift of mindful magic and light". Flames of fire leap from the lamp and out pops a young boy.

"Welcome my friend to this magical journey of mindful magic, mindful ways to stir up your life and bring magic your way. Come and see my earthly friend, a magic road to the crock of gold." The genie waved the boy over. "Have a look, my friend. Look right to the end. The road is magic and will bring you ups and downs, but trust me, you will receive at the end of the road, the crock of gold," said the genie.

"Hey, did you say crock of gold? I am interested. I cannot wait for this adventure; it sounds exciting, and I might die of curiosity. So, it might be a good idea to take this on board and see what is there for me," said the young boy to himself.

He is thoughtful for a moment, with his finger pressed against his lips.

"What could it be that you have for me?" he demanded.

"Before we begin, what is your name?" asks the genie.

"My name is George. Do you know the nursery rhyme Georgie Porgy?" he questioned.

"No, but I would love to hear it," replied the genie.

George straightens his shoulders, brushed back his hair and began, "Georgie Porgy pudding and pie kissed the girls and made them cry. When the boys came out to play, Georgie Porgy ran away."

"My friends tease me by singing this to me all the time," said George.

George goes on to tell the genie.

"That is me, you see. I do not spend too much time pampering girls. I love them and leave them. They are too much hassle and demand a lot of stuff. I am a busy guy. I've have been running around doing my chores and my schoolwork.

"I also have a job delivering newspapers and leaflets to doors after school. It is okay. It does not pay me much and to be honest, people throw them in the bin. So, I cannot see the purpose of it at all. All the printing and paper waste and people's time, but who cares, they pay me, so that is fine. I need the bucks to help me with food and clothes, and I get the odd games that I like to play. So, you say this magic will help me for sure, and this will bring me to the crock of gold? By the way, what is your name?" asks George.

My name is Silver Lining. "Thanks for telling me all about you," said the genie.

"Are you serious? Silver Lining?" says George "Bahahaha! I cannot stop laughing! What kind of name is that? Hi Ho Silver Lining! I know a song with that line in it. I cannot remember the songwriter or singer. Would you like to hear it?"

"Yes, of course, I would love to hear it. It would be my pleasure," responded Silver Lining.

"I have a good talent to sing a song, play a tune, and dance along. So here it goes," said George.

George straightens his hair, pulls his shoulders back and shifts his hips from side to side. He opens his mouth wide and starts to sing as he moves around in circles dancing and clapping his hands.

"Hi Ho Silver Lining, anywhere you go now baby, I see your sun is shining, but I will not make a fuss, though it is obvious… HAAHAAHHAAHHAA. You are supposed to shine like the sun. Get real, Genie Lining. My jaws are sore from laughing. Bahahaha!" George falls to the ground, laughing, holding his belly as the pain shrieked through him with laughter rippling through his body like a tornado.

"I love it when I laugh like this!" shouted George. "It is a tonic". Eventually, George stopped and got up off the ground.

"Come on, show me, show me, I cannot wait to see what is there for me," said George as he waved his hands around in the air.

"That was wonderful, George, very entertaining. Thank you so much. You are quite a singer and dancer!" said the genie. "But now we must see what lies ahead. I have important information for you."

"You make it sound so mysterious. Spit it out," huffed George

The genie went on. "Believe and trust this way, for it will help your whole life through. Be present right here, right now. There is only now. This will bring you a life full of memories and peace, a magical place just to be. A life of present moments, remembering what you do, and this will create memories for you even if these moments are sad too. That is okay; it is not nice, but it is part of life. Life is not a bed of roses, so let us keep rising and keep going; that is the spirit, my boy.

"You are right here right now, not running from the past or yesterday's woes with thoughts that take you back to the past or into the future and keep you on the worry train as you go round and round in circles. *Let it go*, step off the train and take a bow and stay here in the moments of today. We can create plans, but we do not know how it will go. So, let us live for the present. You will be looked after, I know," said the genie.

I will be looked after, or so you say," said George doubtfully. "Are you sure?" he asked.

"That is right; everything will be alright. The crock of gold is waiting for you. Trust and believe, and you will find it. You will receive abundance in all ways, joy, peace, contentment, and love. A life full of adventures and lots of fun, not just for you but for everyone," said Silver Lining.

The genie looks super confident and speaks with a very encouraging voice. He looks at George with loving eyes and genuinely wants to help this earthly boy to find a better way of living life.

George stands up and hollers, "I cannot wait for the gold that will generate money just for me, then I can please myself easily," and he laughs out loud. Bahahaha!

CHAPTER 2

THE MAGIC LAMP

Silver Lining smiles at George and stands up tall as he pushes his shoulders back. He holds the lamp in his hand, and as he rubs it gently, steam begins to pour from its spout. The genie calls out loud.

"Magic and light, fire so bright, show us the way of how to be, to have a life of love and peace. A life of happiness just for me, full of abundance in every way. Being financially supported and looked after well, with joy and people who share that love, happiness comes as we live in the present. Show me the mindful magic for everyone."

In the next instant, out pops the words ***Focus, Attention, Concentration, Notice***.

The genie holds the lamp lovingly to his heart.

"Thank you, dear lamp, for the gifts you bring. Now I must bring them to George as I sing." The genie sets the lamp down, takes one foot forward, clears his throat, and begins to sing.

"Number one – ***attention***. Pay attention to all that you do, including when washing and dressing and listening too. So, when you go outside, pay attention to all around you.

"Number two – ***focus***. Focus on the task at hand; one thing at a time is all that is asked.

"Number three – ***notice***. When you bring your attention to the moment you have, you will notice everything around you and within you.

Number four – ***concentration***. Concentrate on one thing at a time. When we concentrate on one thing, we cannot be doing other things. Give it a go, and this will bring you to the crock of gold." The genie stops singing, takes a deep breath in, and exhales out a big puff of smoke.

George cannot believe what he is seeing. He is gobsmacked. *Smoke puffing from his mouth; how weird is that*? George thinks, looking puzzled.

"That means I must take notice of when I have a hole in my sock, and when my belly is hurting, and my jumper is on back to front. I pay attention to what I am doing and stay with one thing at a time. That is the way. I'll concentrate on what I am doing right now, and this helps me do a better job of that task. Is that right, Silver Lining?" asks George.

"You have got it, *stay positive*," replied Silver Lining.

"That is a lot of things to do in one day, but with this magic for me, it's easy-peasy!!!" George exclaims excitedly. "Cheers, genie. I'll give it a go, and that will bring me closer to the crock of gold." George says as he smiles and rubs his hands together contently.

CHAPTER 3

CRAZY WAY, CRAZY DAY

The alarm rings off as a beautiful song from the sea fills the room. It is time to get up, rise, and shine, with sounds of the sea filling the room.

Oh no, it is that time again. George reaches to find his phone to mute the alarm as it continues blaring.

"I've got sleep in my eyes, and I am still tired, but I have just remembered I must start the day the mindful way. I am going to have a great day today; mindful magic is coming my way. I must use my focus and concentration and make the intention to notice what is happening and what I am doing and stay positive," said George to himself.

"Are you up, George?" Mum calls.

"Yes, mum, it's 7 o'clock," replies George.

"Do not forget to brush your teeth and put a coat on, it's cold outside, and we do not want you to get the flu," said Mum.

"Okey-dokey," he responds.

George has a habit of talking to himself with a dialogue of questions and answers.

My teeth are yucky, and my breath smells. I must brush them now before I stink the place out, and no one will speak to me again, thought George.

"Hey, mum! I am saving for a game for the PlayStation. I hope to have enough money by the end of the month," said George.

"That is okay, George, if you give me the housekeeping money for bread and milk, the rest is yours. You are a good lad doing your best and making a few bobs for the house and the rest," said Mum

"Gee, thanks, mum. Nice to know I can get a gift for myself with the leftover cash."

George sees his phone on the bed and picks it up. He notices the time.

"Oh no, I am late. It's 7.05; I must dive!" shouts George.

George spots a bag of crisps and a chocolate bar on the shelf. "That will do," he says and shoves it into his pocket as he takes his jacket and his rucksack and heads for the door.

"George, have you had your breakfast?" yells Mum.

"Yes, mum! I must go. Bye for now," he said and shut the door behind him.

As George walks along the pathway to the shop where he picks up newspapers, he takes the chocolate bar from his pocket and begins to eat. George had been gifted a phone by his rich uncle, who had so many he gave one away. It worked well, but George did have problems with the buttons now and then. He checked the phone for any messages and clicked into a YouTube channel to listen to his all-time favourite tracks. It was a track from the 1960s and his favourite band, *The Beatles*—unusual taste for an 11-year-old boy whose friends loved rap or dance music. George munches on the crisps, which he likes to eat together with chocolate. As he approaches the shop, his stack of newspapers is waiting. He pops them into the bag, and off he goes on his usual route as he delivers the daily papers and leaflets of many descriptions. As he makes his way, he plays on his phone, eats his breakfast, and in between all that, sends a text to his friend.

George's head is full of questions. This is the normal stuff that happens every day for George. He had sent a text yesterday to his friends Karl, John, Martin, and Maria to ask them about the get together after school today. George received no answer, so he begins to think as he goes on his paper round. *But no one has texted me? I wonder why? I feel worried.*

Did I do something wrong, or maybe they are beginning a new song and did not invite me along? Another thought forms to remind him of his exam, which is today, and he is sure he will fail. Another thought passes his mind about his football match tomorrow. His feelings and thoughts say no.

I do not want to play, but I suppose I will have to show up anyway. George remembers his manager telling him he was on the side-line collecting balls because his training was not up to scratch at all. The thoughts pounded around inside George's head.

As George continues pondering all the different thoughts, he remembers mindful magic. I am doing my chores, but my thoughts are with me as I go. The day pretty much went this way until he retired home at the end of the day feeling wrecked. His head was fuzzy, dizzy, and foggy, and he did notice his legs ached.

George went straight to his bedroom and lay down on the bed. He felt angry and betrayed by Silver Lining. When George feels angry, he lets it out. He shouted to the top of his voice.

"Silver Lining, where is the magic you promised me? Nothing has happened. Only my thoughts stayed with me; such crazy lies you fed to me. Silver Lining, you are in trouble with me. You fool!!!"

His mother heard the shouts and called, "George, are you okay? Who are you talking to, George?"

"No one, mum," he answered.

"George, I heard you. Stop calling people fools. Who has upset you?" she demanded.

"It's okay, mum, honestly. It is just me being silly, practising being angry," said George.

"Give it up, George," his mum said.

CHAPTER 4

WHEN THE GOING GETS TOUGH

Silver Lining magically appears, holding the lamp and calling out.

"Love and flow come to me. Magic and spice and all things nice, my friend George, I am back to help your magic to flow mindful ways to the crock of gold. My dear friend, George, how are you? I hope the magic has happened for you?" asks Silver Lining.

"Are you joking? Are you trying to make fun of me? I am so angry with you I could thump you. You are a liar, and your pants are on fire. You told me to do all those things, and nothing happened, no magic for me. This magic is a joke, and you are for sure a liar, sending me round in a whirlwind. I was upside down running around. Topsy, turvy all over the place, and my thoughts kept taking me to another place. I am exhausted from all the things that I must do and my worries about them too. I am worse than ever. You have put a spell of evil on me. The devil's tricks," shouted George.

"Any more devilish ways and I'll thump *you* back to your never-never land of hopeless dreams," screamed George.

"You tell me, genie, what your stupid lamp has for me now. More tricks and lies for sure!!! Where is the gold you promised me? Show me! It is just a waste of time for me. I am up to my eyes with these so-called moments. It is making me dizzy."

"I feel sick," wails George. He falls to the ground, feeling overwhelmed and incredibly stressed.

George faints.

"Oh, poor boy! Let me see; I have just the right thing here magically. Stay calm, stay cool," says the genie. He pulls out a tube of smelling salts. "Come on, George, now wakey wakey! Waving it around, he puts it under his nose.

"Ah, there you are! Sit up now, back straight against the wall, and it will support you easily. Well done, you are here right now."

"Oh, my head!" cried George. "I need a drink. I am dehydrated from running all over the place and listening to you and this nonsense about mindful magic."

"Here, my friend, just for you a magic potion of magic brew," said Silver Lining.

"Gee, thanks. Give me a whirl; I am thirsty," said George.

"It is made of herbs and spice and all things nice to give you energy day and night. Take it. An energiser, a booster too, to help you focus on what you must do," said Silver Lining.

"Okay, I've got nothing to lose. I need some energy today, and I am not doing so well in any way," George mused.

Silver Lining hands him the drink, and he drinks it fast and furiously.

"Slow down George, you move too fast, you've got to make it last," said Silver Lining.

"It went down in lumps, but I still got the taste of it. It was like sweet chocolate-coated marshmallows. Have you any leftovers? I could down it once more, that is, if you have you any more?" Laughed George.

"Oh no, one potion is all you need for sure," replied Silver Lining.

"It is a natural tonic to help you improve your energy and health," Silver Lining informed him.

"Listen, my friend, I hear you. I understand how you must feel with no energy left as you move upside down on the train of worry without space to rest. I am sending love and compassion to you right now," said Silver Lining.

"What! are you nuts? Why would you do that? Love for me?" yelled George.

"I do not want your love. I do not need your schemes, tricks, or lies. I want my crock of gold right now!" he screams.

CHAPTER 5

ATTITUDES THAT BRING MAGIC

"Hold on, my dear friend. Look at the Lamp. It is rocking from side to side. More information for you to receive," Silver Lining clapped in excitement. The lamp hops around in circles. It shakes from side to side and makes lots of noises. Suddenly the lamp starts to speak, and the words flow out – *Acceptance, Patience, Beginner's Mind*, and *Trust*.

"These mindful attitudes here are four, in time there will be more," squeaked the lamp. The lamp then belches loudly and settles onto the floor.

"Thank you, my dear lamp. You never let me down, magical things happen when you are around," said the genie with a twinkle in his eye.

He smiles so wide that George feels the energy the smile brings, and it emanates all over the room. George's hair stands up on his head, his shoulders relax, and he feels calm.

Silver Lining stands tall and speaks.

"My dear George, *acceptance!* Accepting the situation for what is happening in the present moment is especially important. So, when you are having difficulties with mindfulness that is okay, be gentle with it. It takes time to make changes. Understand that is okay too. When your energy is low, take note and rest to let your energy flow." Silver Lining advised.

"Next, we have **_patience_**. Being patient is a learning curve; there are lots of bumps in the road. That is the way it goes. I will give you tools to help you see ways to ride over them easily.

"Next is **_beginner's mind_**. See this as a new way to be. Look at it with fresh eyes as you see new beginnings and a fresh start. Think about how exciting it feels when you look at the bright side of life. Count your blessings. See all the things you have in your life. The little things that you do or say can mean the most. Practice them every day. With patience, this will happen in time, and you will receive," Silver Lining said in a gentle tone.

"**_Trust!_** Trust in the journey; it is a new way. It may not be the way you think it should be, but a plan lies ahead, wait and see. It will bring you blessings of many kinds, ones that will last a lifetime," laughs the genie, who takes one turn and disappears.

"What is he laughing at?" George was puzzled.

"More of the same nonsense," he scoffed.

Acceptance, patience, beginner's mind, and trust. More ways for me to look at me! Trust in the journey, although it may not turn out the way I think, George wrestled with his thoughts.

"Well, I am not happy about that. I want my crock of gold, and so I must accept this way right now. Whatever happens is okay, it will bring me to the crock of gold. That is a lot to take in, and where do I begin?" George thought aloud.

He promptly lies down, pulls the blanket over his head, and falls asleep.

Silver Lining reappears in a flash of light with chimes and ringing a bell.

"My dear George, wakey wakey, pay attention. Rise and shine, it is time to learn more mindful magic, listen to the chimes. You will need it now as you go on the journey. This is an important message for you." Silver Lining holds a scroll and begins to read the message.

"You must understand. Let me explain. Thoughts will come, thoughts will go, and it is okay when this happens, just bring yourself back to the flow. It is just your old habits taking hold. Trust me, I know because I have been there many times. I just keep bringing myself back to the moment. This is the way it goes," said Silver Lining as he continues.

"The flow, my friend, is your task at hand. Whatever you do, the more you stay present, magic will happen for you. But remember, you are in charge; you decide what to do, one thing at a time is all that is asked. One thing at a time."

Silver Lining blows a trumpet to signal the end of his message.

"Stop! My ears, you fool!" George shouted.

The genie disappears in a cloud of dust.

George begins to pace the floor because this is what he does when he is anxious. He walks up and down, in and out of circles, pacing the floor and then decides to take a walk to clear his head. He walks down by the river, where he notices ducks flapping in the water.

So, he says thinking is part of me. Of course, I know that if I did not think my brain would be dead. There would be no plans, and nothing would happen for me. He is telling me something I already know, thought George.

"He says it is my habit of old that keeps me in this thinking mode. Now it is all about bringing me back to the present moment. I am walking now. My foot hurts, and my chest is tight. Okay, I am noticing things about me. Look, I just saw a monkey and chimpanzee swinging happily from tree to tree. This is not easy," screams George.

Suddenly, Silver Lining appears and says, "I am here to help you along. Let us be friends and listen to what I must tell you. After all, I am here to help you."

"Whatever!" George responded.

The genie looks lovingly at George and says, "A positive mind is to be kind to yourself and tell yourself you can do it too. When you notice you have wandered off in thinking and worries and questions flood your mind, bring yourself back a thousand times. With a gentle wave, just say *stop, look, listen*, that is a mindful magic trick. It will bring you back to the moment you are in. It is as simple as that, but it is up to you, the genie said to the lad.

"One other thing, you take the reins. That is right; it is up to you to be intentional about putting in the work because effort is key. No excuses open to the moment and you will receive. You are in charge; the choice is yours. You can bring yourself back to the moment for sure!" Silver Lining disappears into a puff of smoke vibrating all colours of the rainbow.

George continues to walk as his thoughts play out in his mind.

*I can do this. It's as simple as that, **but** it takes effort. Oh, I'm not so sure if I want to try this at all, it changes my life from the way I know, but maybe that way is not the way to go,* he pondered.

The one thing I'm sure of is that I need to find my crock of gold. If this is the way, I must keep going on that road. I cannot give up or run away, as I tend to do that every day. I must keep going to get my gold. I need it so badly. It will make me rich, and I can have all the things in my life that I want. A big house full of riches and friends around me, a pool that I can swim in, servants to wait on me, food at my call, parties galore and lots of fun day and night, no worries, or cares for the day. One last thing, I will write my own songs and play my guitar while singing along. I want a contract for my music and songs and a band where we can play till the dawn. I can have everything I want. I will just keep walking on the road to get to the crock of gold, thought George.

CHAPTER 6

BUILDING THE MAGIC BLOCKS

Silver Lining reappears, feeling fantastic and rubbing his lamp. "Hello, George, more messages for you. I am so excited to bring more mindful ways to live each day. Bubbly love, bubbly light bring George more mindful sights," said the genie. Out spills the words, *Learning, Making Mistakes, and Effort.*

George finds a bench to sit by the river. There is a grassy patch with a beautiful Oak tree. The genie sits down by the tree and begins. "Making mistakes helps us grow. We learn each day; we expand as we go. Our brain makes room for more to fit in, new ways to do things, and happiness begins. There is one more thing I must tell you," he said, holding a light bulb in his hand. "Your brain will awaken, and you will see new ways to do things and be open to your creativity. When we make mistakes, it is a learning tool, so when we accept life as it is, we find new ways to do things and new ways to be. Life is a sea of whatever we want it to be.

"Trying is important too because when we try to give our time and our energy to our projects and plans, we will receive a reward. Understand that when we try, happy feelings arrive. I have something for you, a heart and a horseshoe," said Silver Lining.

The genie flew around in circles, dipping and diving, and left the horseshoe and heart on the bench as he disappeared.

How nice, thought George. "He gives me a heart and a horseshoe. It makes me feel special, but not for long, as my thoughts begin to crowd me one by one," he said aloud.

"What a list of junk I must take in, making mistakes, learning, and trying. I am sick of it all. It is making me tired, and I am starving."

The boy searches his pockets and finds crisps and a bar of chocolate. He eats them like a savage as the chocolate smudges all over his face.

Silver Lining appears again. "My dear friend if you listen, you will learn. If you open your heart to see, hear, feel, and touch. The five senses around you will bring you a lot."

The genie leaves a magic box in front of George and disappears.

"Oh, what is this? It looks amazing. I wonder what is in here. Wow!" George exclaimed as his eyes take in the sight of shining diamonds and crystals all over the box.

Feeling a little nervous, he reaches to open the box.

He takes a breath, opens the lid and leaps away from the box. Out jumps a pair of eyes, a pair of ears, a mouth, a nose, a pair of hands, and a heart.

The eyes dance and twinkle and speak. "Look around and take notice of all you see, savour the moment completely."

"So, when my thoughts intrude, I must start noticing things. I look around and see everything around me. Is that right?" asks George

"Yes, that is right. When you begin to overthink, just focus and notice with your eyes the beauty around you, the places and people who surround you," replied the eyes with a twinkle.

The eyes close and slide back into the box.

The ears jump out next. They dance, vibrate and speak.

"Listen carefully to all that you hear, it is a way to learn; when we listen to others, we learn a lot. Listen to another and lend an ear to attentively hear from your heart as well," said the ear pulsing in and out.

"Wow, so I must pay attention to what I hear in conversations with my parents, my teachers, my friends. If I listen to other people and what they have to say I can learn from that. Listening to another from my heart, what do you mean from my heart? I listen with my ear," quizzed George.

The ears dance and laugh.

"That is right; you are on the right track. Everyone on this earth has a beautiful heart, but they must tune in. You are a clever one now that you know you can listen to yourself through your heart, check in and see how you feel. Deep down, you have this heartfelt feeling to connect to another. Listen and offer your presence with a smile or a kind word to help. Listen to your heart with understanding. This way, you will know how to have empathy for yourself and another—offering your time and opening the space to be with yourself. What you say to yourself matters. Use kind words and gentle ways to be kind to yourself as you go on your way. Kindness starts with you, and when this happens, you can be kind to others too. A kind word, a kind action, and a kind deed," says the ear laughing.

"Oh, I thought that was why Silver Lining gave me the heart. One more question. What does empathy mean?"

The ears begin to dance again, and George watches with rapt attention. "It means putting yourself in someone else's shoes and understanding how they feel, and that includes you. So, when the going gets tough, and you feel worn out, sad, angry, moody, understand these emotions come and go, they do not stay around unless you want them to," the ear said to the puzzled boy.

George starts laughing!

"Putting myself in someone else's shoes would be hard. I wear a size 1. I have small, tiny feet and twinkly toes.

I am fussy with shoes, not everything suits," George informed the ears still laughing.

"Okay Gotcha! In other words, understanding how someone else is feeling today?" George asked.

"That is right, lad, you hit it on the head," laughed ears.

"Someone may feel, sad, worried, angry, anxious or nervous, and these emotions come and go, they do not stay. No one knows what anyone is going through. So, understand how others might feel. And that includes me. Oops, almost forgot that," George said sheepishly.

"You are a smart boy, George," said ears.

"Well, I am in a situation right now myself. It is one with Silver Lining. He is taking me around in circles, promising me a crock of gold. I am not getting anywhere; I'm only noticing my worries more. I am listening to you, ears. I hear you! That is the magic, so I am told, but I really need the crock of gold!" yells George.

The ears stop, move back, and drop into the box.

In that split second, the nose vibrates, leaps out and begins to speak. "Hey, look boy take note of all the smells around you – nice ones and not so nice. They are all part of life," snorts the nose.

"That is so true, some smells are disgusting," said George, wrinkling his nose. I do not like the smell of rubbish bins or silage; it makes me feel sick, and the fishy smell stinks. I love the sweet and earthy fragrance of beautiful flowers and trees. I will have fun smelling my way through the day." George watches nose curiously.

"What have you next?" he questioned.

Nose disappears into the box and out pops mouth dancing and singing.

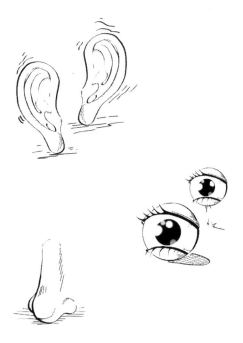

"Please taste the tender, succulent flavours of food and drinks that you drink. Chew slow, swallow easy, and chew it all. Gobbling it up takes the good out of it," said the mouth

"Okay, I am guilty," George exclaims and throws his hands in the air, "This makes sense. I rush my food that is so true. I eat it so quickly that I do not taste it at all, and I am always looking for more; it goes in one go. I am always in a hurry rushing to the next thing I must do. My schedule is busy all over the place, so I must keep up with the pace.

"I am starving most of the time, taking snacks out of my pockets to keep me going. A sugar rush, woosh! So, slowing down is the key. That way, I will taste my food and fully enjoy my meal," said George feeling happy and much more confident. "Thanks so much for your advice, I will give it a go sugar and spice," said George.

George watches as the mouth opens and closes and disappears into the box. Suddenly, out flies the hands as they dance and sing and wave about.

"Hello, I am glad you can see me now. I can touch and feel my hair, my skin, almost anything at all; it is a wonderful way to feel today. You can use your hands, yes you can. The touch of your hands on many things tells you a lot about things. What joy it can bring. You can also shake hands with another, and this way we befriend each other."

The hand stretches to shake George's hand.

"Hey buddy," said the hand

George takes his hand from his pocket and reaches out, wraps his hand into the other hand. The hand gives George a good, warm shake.

George feels more comfortable after that and for some reason, feels happier inside.

"Yes, that is true; my hands help me in all the things I do," said George. "I like writing songs, eating, dressing myself and washing too. My hands practically do everything for me. What would I do without my hands? I am not sure how I would feel. They are a gift to me. I know a song about hands, would you like to hear it? I don't know the name of the songwriter or singer."

"Sure, why not. Give me a bell," said the hands.

"Okay, it goes like this." George pulls his shoulders back, moves his hips and straightens his hair. He opens his mouth wide and sings, "Hands up baby hands up, give me your heart give me, give me your heart, give me, give me, hands up, baby hands up, give me your heart, give me, give me me your heart give me, give me, all your love, all your love."

He moves around dancing, shaking his hips and throwing his hands up in the air. When he is finished, he turns to face the hands.

"That is it. What do you think?" he asked.

"Quite nice, George, you have a great voice," hands answered.

"Ah, thanks, it's natural, my grandfather was a singer too. It is in the family," George declared as he brushed his hands through his hair and lifted his head feeling immensely proud.

While George is catching his breath after exerting himself with the dance, a heart leaps in front of him smiling, jumping, and laughing as it moves.

It addresses the boy. "I stand in this powerful glow of love, joy, and peace. If you stand on this bridge of love, you will flow. Tap into your heart, you know the truth lies in you," said the heart.

George is fascinated as he watches the heart leap and jump. "What do you mean the truth lies in me?"

"Pay attention to how you feel? Tapping into your heart will help you see the truth of everything around you," replied the heart

"Okay, my thoughts are not important right now. Tune into my heart, and it will tell me a lot. Okey dokey," said George. "Thanks a lot. I'll give it a go." George makes to leave and walk back home.

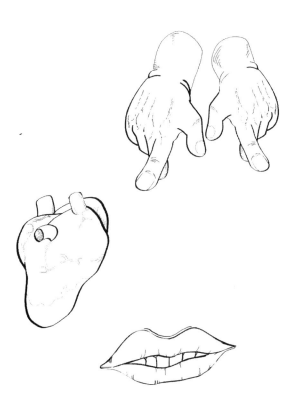

Just before he leaves, he turns towards the heart and speaks, "Okay, I can give my love to others each day by listening to my heart in a particular way," said George.

George takes the heart and the horseshoe that Silver Lining gave him out of his pocket. He stands on one foot holding the heart in one hand and the horseshoe in another and begins to recite, "I will stand on the bridge of love and light even if I wobble, maybe my friends will appear to hug and kiss me here. Ohhhhhh noooooooooooo!"

George topples over.

CHAPTER 7

LIGHT BULB MOMENT

"Wow. Thank you, my friends, for reminding me of the gifts that I have already with me. Now I will take notice and use them fully," said George.

"Yes, that is right. No doubts or excuses along the way, stay with the moments of the day," said the genie.

"Hey, thanks, Silver Lining, I will tune in to the senses. I have my gifts for life, and it is important to see it this way. Mindful magic coming my way. I will not forget as my thoughts arise; I will bring myself back a thousand times," George added.

"You are amazing, George," Silver Lining declared, feeling immensely proud of the boy.

"Believe in yourself, because you are, for sure, a precious gem. Magic happens when you believe in you," said Silver Lining, and he leapt in the air and disappeared.

George walked home, feeling incredibly happy and contented with all he had learned.

This will bring me closer to the crock of gold, he thought.

The following morning, George wakes up to the sound of chimes like sweet celestial music in his ears.

The genie sings. "Rise and shine; it is the time to rise to begin the day the mindful way."

George peeps out from under the blanket to see Silver Lining dressed in a vibrant bright coloured suit with jingles and jangles hanging from it. They play beautiful music as the genie moves in the air, filling George's ears with harmonious sounds.

"Is it not a bit early for this kind of stuff?" George demanded.

Silver Lining smiled and answered, "See the bright side of life, George. I have another magic trick for you, my dear friend."

"You mean, there is more?"

The genie took one breath in and out as he moved gracefully from one side of the room to the next. He asked the chimes to close their mouths and be quiet as he spoke. "My breath is the life that has been given to me; a natural thing that's part of me. I am blessed and looked after eternally," said the genie.

George watched as the genie inhaled and exhaled big breaths that looked like clouds as he flew around.

The genie turned to look at him. "This helps me to be and connects me to that space that is within me. It also gives me lots of energy. Watch me!"

The genie flew around the room effortlessly with a beautiful big smile across his face. He floated from corner to corner, taking nice breaths in and out. The more breaths he took, the easier he flew. Round and round from corner to corner as he dipped in and out waving to George as he passed by.

George watched and asked the genie, "What do you want me to do, Silver Lining?"

"My earthly friend, I want you to use your breath with grace and ease, and this way you can reconnect with yourself. You were born with your breath, the giver of life. It is there for a reason to connect you back into the moment you're in." The genie laughs out loud as he continues to soar around the room. "Get up out of bed and stand tall so you can practice this breathwork for a moment."

George peels the blanket back and stands on the floor. "Okay, I am ready, my feet are on the floor, and I am standing up tall."

"Let us begin. Take a nice breath in and let it out. Nice and easy does it, George. Focus on the breath as it moves in and out. Feel the rise and fall of your chest or belly as it moves in and out. Paying attention to the breath, place your hand on your belly to feel it rise," said Silver Lining.

George begins to breathe in and out with his hand on his belly. He notices his breath flow and his hands rising and falling in rhythm. He breathes faster.

"Slow down, George, slow and steady wins the race."

As George breaths in and out, it seems to be taking a lot of effort on his part. He continues to breath faster and faster until his breath goes into rapid breathing.

"SLOW DOWN GEORGE," the genie calls out in a loud voice.

"Faster and faster, I go in and out, oh no, I am feeling lightheaded. Gee-whiz," says George as he collapses onto the bed.

The genie quickly scoots down from the corner of the room to assist him. "Are you okay?"

"Just about," said George said, opening one eye.

"George, you must slow down. That is the key you will find honestly." Silver Lining vanishes.

George feels a little overwhelmed but realises now that all his senses connect him to the present moment. They are an incredible way to greet the day.

"My breath is a great way to connect to me as I bring myself back to the moment *I breathe*. They are with me as I work and play. I need to connect and use them fully so I can benefit from the moments around me." George muttered in the empty room.

He gets dressed, paying attention to his flow of thoughts as he tries to bring himself back to what he is doing in the present, which is dressing himself. He has a habit of putting his jumper on back to front, not noticing till usually, his mum brings his attention to it. He realises this had happened again and takes it off to put it on the correct way. He gathers his belongings, puts them into the bag and watches them going in one by one. He notices a pattern of old thoughts coming to his mind and making way for more thoughts.

These thoughts are concerns about the future and worries about how he would pass his exam the next week. George immediately remembered Silver Lining saying use the magic word concentrate. So, George did not try to get rid of the thought; he simply turned his attention to what he was doing right at that moment.

CHAPTER 8

MINDFUL MAGIC IN PLAY

George grabs his coat and makes his way to the newspaper shop to pick up his newspapers for delivery. While walking, he decides not to use his phone because Silver Lining said one thing at a time was all that he needed. He opens up to his five senses and notices the sounds of birds as he walks, how beautifully they chirp and tweet happily. He also hears the traffic buzzing by and the nose of a tractor in the distance. He feels the wind brush his face and smells the scent of sweet flowers as he catches a glimpse of colourful geraniums when he passes by a beautiful garden on the way to the shop. He had never noticed all these before because he was too busy thinking and completely distracted by his phone and a YouTube channel.

George realises that his toe hurts, so he stops to take his runner off and have a look to see what is happening. He notices a cut on the bottom of the foot exactly right under his big toe.

Those darn football boots have done it again. I may buy a new pair, they are ill-fitting around my toe and have caused damage, and it is sore, thought George. "OUCH!" He yelled. George pulled a tissue from his pocket, wrapped it around his toe, pulled the sock back up and put his foot back into his runner.

He continues his day, bringing himself back from his distracting thoughts to focus on his daily routine, doing one thing at a time, and staying in the flow.

George did notice that his thoughts kept returning, but he just gently accepted they were there and chose to focus on what he was doing instead. The more he did this, the more he did not notice the thoughts as much. The thoughts did not carry him away because he was focused on his task.

They came and went just like clouds in the sky; they passed by and did not bother George in any way. George had a new plan to focus on the task at hand.

Wow! Thought George. *What a new way for me. I am truly taking charge of my life, and I am experiencing the day differently.*

He returned after a day of work and school, feeling lighter, brighter and happier.

After his dinner, he retired to bed, and suddenly he felt a gush of warm air fill the room. A cloud of smoke settled on the ceiling, and the genie appeared with the lamp.

"Hello, my dear friend, George. How is the mindful magic going?" He danced with the lamp, waving it around and smiling like a Cheshire cat.

George looked up with a big smile on his face. "I cannot believe it!" He squealed. "I practised everything you said, and it helped me to be with the moments of my day that usually just run away. My thoughts are now in the background, and I can step forward and take the reins. As you said, I am in charge, and I am no longer thinking as much. I can see and remember things that I do. I do not have to double-check everything I do. I noticed my jumper was back to front, a habit I had for months," said George.

"I am incredibly happy for you. Once you decide to follow the advice magic happens, that is right," said Silver Lining.

"Now, before you go, I must ask you what my goal and purpose are to find the gold. This way for me will set me free," said George.

Silver Lining stopped dancing, flew to the floor, and placed the lamp in front of George. "More mindful magic for you today," laughs Silver Lining.

The lamp began to splutter as its spout stretched out so long and it made a choking sound.

"Are you okay?" George looked at the lamp with worry etched on his face.

The lamp made several choking sounds and out spluttered a puff of smoke, which vanished to reveal a flapping winged dove. The dove dipped and dived around the room and made its way to a bookshelf where he perched. There, he let his feathers down and relaxed his wings by his side.

"I cannot believe my eyes. It gets better every day. What have you to say?" George asked.

The dove began, "I am here to bring you hope, and to give you a blessing of love and peace. This interaction with yourself and others will be all you need. So, when you see a dove, you can be sure it is me bringing blessings from above," squawked the dove.

The bird took one jump from the shelf soared around beautifully in front of George. He suddenly stopped still and looked with a deep gaze into the boy's eyes. George was perplexed.

"Remember me," he said, and suddenly, a loud bang, a puff of smoke, and he was gone.

George took a deep breath to steady himself after the encounter.

CHAPTER 9

NEW WAYS TO BE

The lamp stepped to the forefront and began to speak. Out flows the words **Letting Go**, **Non-Striving**, **Non-Judging**, **Gratitude**, *and* **Generosity.**

"More mindful ways to help you today. More knowledge, you see, and you are coming to the end of the road after these," the lamp said in a hoarse voice.

"So how will these help me?" asked George.

The lamp straightens it spout and speaks.

"*Letting go*! Letting go of your old habits, thought patterns that do not help, which just bring you to more muddle and stir up trouble. Let them go and find the new way to be, this will bring you joy and peace forever," said the lamp

"That is true; my thoughts can get me into trouble," answered George. "It can make me angry if I think no one cares, especially my friends. Also, when I think and do not trust anything they say or do. My thoughts can also get weird if I get carried away making scenarios that are not in play," said George.

"The next one for you is **Non-Striving**," said the lamp. "This mindful attitude is a special one. We try so hard to reach our goals, our achievements, and plans. We plan every day, but not everything works out as we plan, and that is okay. We put ourselves under a lot of pressure, pushing and shoving all over the place, missing the fun of life as it plays." The lamp coughs as the words sputter all over the place.

George watches in amusement, as the lamp swings from side to side.

The lamp clears its throat and continues. "The attitude of non-striving gives us space to see things. It opens us up to more clarity, bringing self-compassion and patience as you walk easily because sometimes our plans die quickly. Life is beautiful, what is the hurry, take the moments of each day, embrace them, and love them every way. What is meant for you will not pass you by. Take it all in your stride as you learn a new way," sputtered the lamp.

"Thanks, that's a lot. Yes, I agree when you say striving too much is not the way because I do put pressure on myself every day. *Listen*, I want to have a good life, not scrimping and scraping money to buy the things I need. You see, I am taking steps to create for myself a future life full of bliss and harmony. I dream of a house and children, with lots of abundance around me too. Okay, so you are telling me my plans *may not* be the ones I planned already? That is horrendous news you have told me today; you have just taken away the good that is coming my way. *My* crock of gold is waiting for me. You can say what you like it is coming alright," said George.

"That is great! Your ideas and inspirations are taking hold. Remember, George, you are making waves for a new way to be, and honestly, this will bring you all the abundance you need. When I say things do not work out as planned, it just means it may not be the plan you had first-hand. A new opportunity will come, rest assured you will receive whatever is best for you as you go on your way," the lamp retorts.

"*Okay,* I am listening," replied George.

"The next one is *Trust.* Accept what comes because it will bring light into your life that you never knew." A big puff of smoke billows from the lamp, it rattles, cough and suddenly stops.

"I will keep going because I am in too deep, and now I see some changes are happening to me. I trust, and I know it is my crock of gold," answers George

The lamp makes one turn to the right side and another one to the left. The lamp speaks. "*Gratitude*! This, George, is a must for you, and this attitude will last your whole life through. It is a gift that can be given to yourself and others, a heartfelt feeling of thanks and appreciation for everything you have and do. Gratitude helps you feel positive emotions, and this way, you can relish and savour good moments. Count your blessing and all you have, remember, the little things mean a lot," says the lamp as he giggles and laughs, hopping around the floor.

"Alright, I hear you. Sometimes I do not see it this way. I focus on all the things I do not have today," answers George.

"Turn your attention the other way. A positive mind brings gratitude your way. See the *blessings* in all things, even things that do not go your way, because they are not meant for you anyway. Look around, open your eyes, and see all you have every day. A grateful heart beats stronger, feels lighter and becomes happier," said the lamp.

The lamp sits quietly, as George takes in what he said. Suddenly, the lamp takes one big belch, and out comes the word *Generosity*. "This means giving back to others, giving your time and money to help others. But do not get me wrong, it is more than money, George, it is about being generous in spirit. This means being kind, considerate, loving and forgiving. So, if someone has wronged you, forgive them and let it go. You may not approve of all their behaviour, but you should let yourself off the hook, so you do not carry the behaviour of another around with you. This sets you free."

The lamp continues to speak.

"Forgive yourself for anything you may have done or not have done. You may have hurt others, so, understand you did your best with the knowledge you had. Now, you'll know more as you expand and grow. Making mistakes is a good part of life because you learn so much. It teaches you lessons to see what you have and offers many choices to do things differently. I hope this helps, George. You will shine so bright, keep up the good work, and remember you are a shining light." The lamp lets out another big belch and stops still.

The genie picks the lamp up, wraps it in a soft, comfy blanket and holds it to his heart.

"I hope you heard the messages from this magic lamp who cares about you and all that you do. You are nearly there keep going, and you will see the crock of gold waiting for you very soon." He took one step backwards and disappeared into a puff of smoke. George sat in a pensive mood until he noticed the smell of sweet roses and lavender fill the room. A calm and peaceful feeling washed over him as he lay down to sleep.

CHAPTER 10

A PLEASANT SURPRISE

George started his day the new way, paying attention as he went on his way. He practised every day, working with his senses and discovered he learned so much about what happened each day, and that he paid attention in an unusual way. His heart felt lighter when he decided to contact a friend he fought with. He told him he was wrong and asked for a chance to be friends again. He thought about all the times he kissed the girls and made them cry and decided that he would show them kindness and treat them right. He would not say horrible things about them; after all, they are somebody's children.

George's heart was taking a big turn. When he realised he had enough money to buy a new game, he decided to buy his mum a perfume and a bun for her tea. She could never afford perfume of any kind since all their money went to paying the bills. They were lucky to have bread and jam.

George got his wages from the newspaper round and decided on the way home to stop by the chemist and buy his mum a perfume. He smelled various ones and decided to go for a sweet flowery smell, which he thought she might like. The good lady wrapped it in lovely flowery paper and put a beautiful pink bow on top. George made his way home. He was a little anxious when he approached the door as he knew his mum would think *what the hell has happened to you?* Again, George realised it was just a thought that may not be true, and so he proceeded towards the door.

He opened the door and walked in. "Hi, mum, I am back," said George.

"Hello, George. How are you doing today?" asks his mum as she stands over the ironing board, ironing clothes.

"I am great. I have a surprise, close your eyes," he said.

"A surprise for me, I cannot wait!" She closed her eyes tightly, purses her lips and waits.

George rummages in his rucksack and finds the gift that the lady kindly wrapped for him in the shop with a beautiful pink bow. Further down, he finds the bun in a bag he bought in the pastry shop with white icing and sprinkles on top.

"Okay, open your eyes, and you will see the magic gift 1, 2, 3," George counts.

Her face fell to the floor. "Oh, dear! George, is this for me? It is not my birthday, that was two months ago."

"Oh yes, I am sorry I am late, but it is better than never. It is for you, for all that you do," said George.

His mother opens the paper excitedly as George watches. Tears flow from her eyes, and she starts to cry. "Thank you so much." She reaches out and gives him a big hug.

George feels awkward and shrugs away. "It's okay, mum."

"What a beautiful gift! I love it. Your generosity will be rewarded, George, honestly. I feel bad because I know you wanted your game."

"I will get that next month. I have enough. I will keep playing the one I have," George answered.

He feels happier now he has given his mum a gift and realises that whatever he has is enough. George goes up to his room and lies in bed.

CHAPTER 11

MORE JINGLE JANGLE

Out of the corner of his eyes, George spots a bright light. It is a star, and it shines so bright. The star moves in the middle of the ceiling and inside the star appears Silver Lining.

"Hi, George, I am here again to give you one last gift, the one you will need for the future. When challenges come, step out this way, this will help you every day."

"What might that be?" asks George. "I am doing much better now that I am finding my feet," he said.

"You stuck with it all. You have the courage and strength of a lion." The genie praised him.

The genie took a crystal out of his pocket and waved it around. He muttered something under his breath, and in the flash of a moment, the crystal opens and out pops a lion. The lion opens his mouth wide and exhales a big sigh, followed by a roar, and he speaks.

"Hello, my name is King Kong," roars the lion.

George smiles.

"Hey, that is a great name for you. It fits perfectly! Look at the size of you." Laughs George. "Hey, King Kong, what is going on?"

The lion roars again and softens his jaw. "Nothing much, just came to check in to see you again. Your courage and strength are flying so high that I think I need to take a nap for a while. You do not need me at all. You have the strength of a lion and ten of my friends, so good luck and believe in your strength, my friend," said the lion.

The lion lies down, lets out one final big roar, and falls asleep.

Silver Lining was sitting cross-legged, suspended in mid-air as he watched from above. He circled his neck from side to side, let out a screech and began to speak. "One more thing for you is to stay still for some days," said the genie.

He pulls a cushion out of his pocket, holds it in one hand and waves the other hand over it. George watches the cushion grow bigger and bigger and bigger. Beautiful trimmings begin to appear and surround the edge with jingling bells. It was golden in colour with red-trimmed edges. Suddenly the genie stops waving his hand and throws it into the air, shouting, "Abracadabra! Magic and light bring George peace all through the night." The cushion whirls around and ends up on top of George's head.

"Hey, what are you doing, silly friend. I cannot see you or hear you under here," George said with humour. "This cushion is heavy and smells like strawberry jelly."

"My dear boy, this is for you to sit on and stay quiet for a little while each day. Finding that quiet space helps you to see that lots of answers will come to you if you take the time to sit, be quiet and rest awhile. This space will bring you lots of abundance and happiness too," said Silver Lining.

"You want me to sit on a cushion and do what, practically nothing? Sounds good to me, I could take this easily every day," George retorted.

"Yes, that's right, I want you to do nothing at all. This time is for you, for your self-care, to rest a while, which will bring you energy and open you to more clarity. You can close your eyes and the same applies when you notice your thoughts, you bring them back a thousand times.

"This time in this place will help you to be. You are not just in motion, *doing things,* but in a still space where you *do nothing*; just be. *This is called meditation*, and it is powerful. Start with five minutes, then increase it to ten, and if you have more time, keep going, my friend," said Silver Lining.

"I am not sure I can do this, but it sounds interesting, and seeing as it is the last straw, I will give it a go." George nodded.

"There have been bumps in the road, but you are learning fast, keep going, your reward is waiting for you," said Silver Lining. He throws George a clear quartz crystal. The sparkling light reflected into George's eyes as it landed in his hand.

"This stone, you can hold in your hand as you sit and feel the warmth and vibration of the light that it brings," said Silver Lining.

"It will help you to focus as you sit, and you will feel it connect to you as you tune in. It is not worth much money now, George. You can never buy what this crystal will bring. It will give you love and harmony as you tune in.

"Meditation will help you make good decisions and clear any clutter you hold in your head. It will be peace and harmony as you sit resting in this light of bliss. If you are tired, you will fall asleep, and that is okay, do not worry, go with the flow because that is what is needed today. Trust in this practice; it is magic and real. It is something that will last you your whole life through," said Silver Lining.

George looks frazzled. *I am tired right now, so maybe I'll give it a go. I need to sleep, so this may help me,* thought George.

The genie smiled down at George, leapt towards the corner of the room, shook his head from side to side, and disappeared.

George set his alarm to finish in five minutes and sat on the cushion. He closed his eyes holding the crystal in his hand and began to feel the warmth coming from the crystal as he sat listening to his breath flowing in and out. Thoughts came and went, and as soon as George noticed this, he brought himself back to focus on his breathing and the sounds around him.

Suddenly, George heard cock a doodle do cock a doodle do. His alarm never let him down. He opened his eyes and reached to turn off the song that brought him back into the room.

"Oh, weird stuff but not bad," he said to the quiet room. *It stops me dead in my tracks and helps me to focus and concentrate. I will stay positive and know that with effort, I will get there. Trying new things is exciting, and after a while, it will be a big part of my routine,* thought George to himself.

He finished his homework and showered, and it was bedtime. He pulled the covers back, and there, sitting on the bed was an envelope with his name written on it. George opened the envelope and found a note saying, "Meet me tomorrow at noon at Dawson Creek. Your partner in crime. Hands up baby, hands up, give me your heart, baby give me your heart." Signed Silver Lining and the magic lamp.

George smiled and felt a warm feeling in his heart as he lay down to sleep.

CHAPTER 12

THE EYE OPENER

Morning arrived with the beautiful sun peering in through the window. George stretched and leapt out of bed because he knew today was the day for the important meeting with Silver Lining and the lamp for possibly the last time. His heart felt heavy because he had enjoyed meeting them even if he never knew when it would happen. It was so random and magical that he did feel rather privileged with these encounters.

Right now, I must stay in the present and enjoy the moment as best I can, thought George. He focused on cleaning his room. He got washed, dressed, and seeing as it was Saturday with no work or school commitments, he told his mum he was meeting his friends at noon and would be back by 3pm.

George made his way to the Dawson creek. A beautiful road leads up to the woodland area of gorgeous trees, flowers, and sweet singing birds. There was a lake there, but no one was allowed to swim due to a drowning incident several years back, after which it was deemed unsafe. The woodland was loved by many, and they all held picnics and outings as they watched the various trees blossom and shed their leaves. The sun was shining as George walked down the road to the end of the creek. There he saw the genie holding a crock of gold, smiling from ear to ear. The lamp was dancing at his feet. Silver Lining put his hand out to shake George's hand.

"Welcome, George, you have finally made it and you deserve your crock of gold. I have it here ready and waiting," said Silver Lining as he shook George's hand.

The heat that came from his handshake was like a hot stone of lava. The vibration ran through George as he received the crock.

"You have received the crock of gold every day by the way you live, laugh, and play. You are fulfilled in many ways; trust me, your life will be abundant, and you'll get all you want when you live by your heart. Yes, do not get me wrong, you will use your head, but you will know deep down what is right and wrong."

George looked at the cauldron but could not see any gold. *For some reason I am not angry*, he thought.

George opened the lid. There he saw crystals of many designs – blue, pink, yellow, orange, black, grey, white, purple, aura light, and all colours of the rainbow. A book with *Mindful Magic* inscribed in beautiful gold writing lay on top of the crystals. George was taken aback as he saw the beautiful crystals dazzling in the pot.

Silver Lining took a scroll from his pocket and began to recite.

"George, I have written you a poem that I want you to keep. I know this will help you to understand all that has been going on. The book in the pot is yours to keep, keeping you on track when you need a read. Is it okay if I read one last poem for you, George?" the genie asked.

"Sure, I've got nothing to lose now only gain. My anger is no longer part of my game," answered George.

George sat down on a rock and waited to hear what the genie had to say.

"It goes like this." The genie clears his throat. "Dear George, I hope you are okay with the outcome today. You see, you have already found the crock of gold each day. The new ways I showed you have helped you live a new way as you take it all in your stride to enjoy every day. You learn to control your anger and react differently when you accept situations around you fully. You are rich in many ways as now you know the feeling of being grateful today. When you get caught up in money and material things, you forget that life is too short and you miss all the rest. Yes, you must have money, a certain amount to keep the roof over your head, and food in the cupboard to keep you fed. Remember, George, you are the guiding light, showing your generosity day and night. What you give out, you will get back; fulfilment and peace will surround you always.

"So, your crock of gold is in your hands. As you use it each day, it will multiply and bring blessings your way. Thank you for listening and taking on board the mindful magic that came your way. The end," said Silver Lining as he takes a bow.

The lamp hops, dances, and jumps around happily as it lets out a puff of smoke and speaks. "George, you are a pleasure to work with. Remember, have fun, dance, and sing because life is too short; enjoy it always." The lamp sputtered and moved from side to side before stopping still. The genie picked it up, wrapped it in a blanket and held it to his heart.

"We must go to another land to find another to help. We have ways to spread this light, ways to help everyone on earth. Mindful magic is the recipe for life," said Silver Lining.

Silver Lining looked lovingly into George's eyes. "I cannot stay, but you never know, I may return someday. Take care of yourself." He leapt into a tree, holding the lamp to his heart. He spun around several times in circles as blue, pink, yellow, green, and purple colours of light shone around him. George watched them intensely until he could no longer see Silver Lining and the magic lamp as they disappeared into dust.

George looked down at his feet, and a bag of crystals and *Mindful Magic* book lay there. He felt a sadness in his heart. Silver Lining was gone. But he also felt immensely blessed to have been given this mindful magic to help spice up his life and bring peace within himself.

George shouted out for all to hear, "I am lucky now that I can see that money will not bring me all the happiness I need. It takes a lot more to create a happy life. This mindful magic I can pass on by the actions I do, I will meditate to bring me through."

He had so much knowledge now of how living life the mindful way with new attitudes would help him each day.

"It is real magic and a new way to be. It brings less stress, less anxiety, less anger and more peace for me," said George.

He picked up the crystal stones, put them into his rucksack along with the book. He brushed his hair back, straightened his shoulders, swayed his hips from side to side, took a leap and a jump, a whistle and a song, as he happily went back home.

Printed in Poland
by Amazon Fulfillment
Poland Sp. z o.o., Wrocław

63371748R00051